Blood Play

Written by
Hannah Bos and
Paul Thureen

Developed by
Oliver Butler

Made by
The Debate Society

SAMUELFRENCH.COM
SAMUELFRENCH-LONDON.CO.UK

FOR PRODUCTION ENQUIRIES

UNITED STATES AND CANADA
Info@SamuelFrench.com
1-866-598-8449

UNITED KINGDOM AND EUROPE
Plays@SamuelFrench-London.co.uk
020-7255-4302

Each title is subject to availability from Samuel French, depending upon country of performance. Please be aware that *BLOOD PLAY* may not be licensed by Samuel French in your territory. Professional and amateur producers should contact the nearest Samuel French office or licensing partner to verify availability.

MUSIC USE NOTE

Licensees are solely responsible for obtaining formal written permission from copyright owners to use copyrighted music in the performance of this play and are strongly cautioned to do so. If no such permission is obtained by the licensee, then the licensee must use only original music that the licensee owns and controls. Licensees are solely responsible and liable for all music clearances and shall indemnify the copyright owners of the play(s) and their licensing agent, Samuel French, against any costs, expenses, losses and liabilities arising from the use of music by licensees. Please contact the appropriate music licensing authority in your territory for the rights to any incidental music.

IMPORTANT BILLING AND CREDIT REQUIREMENTS

If you have obtained performance rights to this title, please refer to your licensing agreement for important billing and credit requirements.

BLOOD PLAY was first produced by The Debate Society and presented by The Bushwick Starr in Brooklyn, NY in October 2012, with scenic design by Laura Jellinek, lighting design by Mike Riggs, sound design by Ben Truppin-Brown, costume design by Sydney Maresca, masks by Jason Leinwand, and properties by Noah Mease. Stage management was by Amy Ehrenberg, production management by Josh Kohler, Producer was Dorit Avganim, Assistant Stage Manager was Shelley Miles and interns were Eileen Casterline, Michael Newton and Shanan Wolfe. It was directed by Oliver Butler. The cast was as follows:

BEV	Hannah Bos
MORTY	Michael Cyril Creighton
GAIL	Birgit Huppuch
IRA	Ronete Levenson
SAM	Hanlon Smith-Dorsey
JEEP	Paul Thureen

During the extension, the role of Ira was played by Jenny Seastone and in subsequent presentations by Emma Galvin. Additional sound design by M.L. Dogg. **BLOOD PLAY** went on to be produced as part of Under the Radar at The Public Theater, The Next Thing Festival at ArtsEmerson and at Williamstown Theatre Festival as part of their 2013 season.

Development and touring of **BLOOD PLAY** was supported by the New England Foundation for the Arts' National Theater Project, with lead funding from the Andrew W. Mellon Foundation.

BLOOD PLAY was developed in part at a Clubbed Thumb/Playwrights Horizons SuperLab and The Bushwick Starr and made possible by grants the Jerome Foundation and the Six Points Fellowship for Emerging Jewish Artists and made possible with major funding from UJA-Federation of New York as well as public funds from the New York State Council on the Arts.

CHARACTERS

BEV FEINBERG – mid 30s, sweet, desperate to fit into the new neighborhood.

MORTY FEINBERG – late 30s, affable, wildly in love with his wife, wants to be a great neighbor.

IRA FEINBERG – 10 years old, fragile and small for his age. An old soul.

SAM FOGELBERG – late 30s, slightly dim but lovable guy's guy.

GAIL FOGELBERG – mid 30s, neighborhood queen bee. Cold. Hard to please.

JEEP MATSON – early 40s, single, odd. Covers his awkwardness with a smile. Walks with a slight, stiff-legged limp.

SETTING

Skokie, Illinois

TIME

Late August. 1951.

To our Grandparents, their children and basements

(A brand new early 1950s basement. Linoleum flooring with a shuffleboard pattern and knotty pine paneling. Close to the ceiling, a window looks out onto the back lawn where a small canvas tent is pitched. It's dusk and a light glows in the tent. Inside the basement, parallel to the back wall on the stage left side is a teal formica-topped bar with bar stools, stocked with full bottles and new glassware. The stage right wall is an Asian-themed mural. Along the wall is a sofa. Stage right is the stairway.)

(Thunder. Darkness on stage. Distant sounds of a campfire and children singing in a round.)

GROUP 1.
> WING AWAY WHIPPOORWILL,
> WING AWAY WEST
> WING AWAY WEST WHIPPOORWILL,
> WING AWAY WEST
>
> *(repeat)*

GROUP 2.
> WHIP-OR-WILL,
> WHIP-OR-WILL,
> WHIP-OR-WHIP-OR-WHIP-OR-WILL.
>
> *(repeat)*

GROUP 3.
> MOUNTAIN LION!

*(**GROUPS** 1 and 2 scream.)*

(The children's playful screams merge into the shrieks of an adult woman.)

BEV. Ahhhhh! Oh my God! Oh God! Oh my God!

(Lights up on the basement bar. Water is spraying from a ceiling pipe. The furniture is soaked. There's a puddle on the floor. The images on the mural are smeared and running.)

BEV. *(cont.)* MORTY! Come down here!

MORTY. *(from upstairs)* What?! Wha wha wha what?!

BEV. OH MY GOD!

(MORTY rushes downstairs.)

It's everywhere! Ohh!

MORTY. Oh my God. The valve. The valve.

(MORTY rushes to the water shut-off valve, standing on a bar stool to reach it. BEV stands on the couch and tries to stop the spray.)

BEV. Oy, look at the mural!

MORTY. No. Noooo!

BEV. I know.

(MORTY turns the valve, the spray slows to a dribble.)

MORTY. BEV, are you ok?

(He goes to BEV, who is soaking wet, and hugs her.)

(investigating the ceiling) There. There's a crack right there.

BEV. I'll get towels. This house. This house is killing me!

(BEV goes upstairs. MORTY looks at the pipe. He gets an ice pick from the bar, climbs up on a chair and starts jamming the ice pick into the cracked pipe. BEV comes back down with towels and puts them on the puddle.)

MORTY. You know it's not so – Oh my God it's bad, it's very bad!

BEV. This is terrible. This is very bad for the tile…and the upholstery.

MORTY. What the heck?

BEV. What?

MORTY. It's a root.

BEV. What?

MORTY. And dirt. There's roots growing in the pipe.

BEV. *(sopping up water, looking at the painting)* Oh my goodness… The Oriental children look like they're melting. The sofa's ruined!

(BEV goes upstairs. MORTY looks at the mural. He's destroyed. He tries to blot it with a rag. He goes back to the pipe.)

MORTY. Bring me a bucket!

BEV. *(from upstairs)* They're all down there.

(MORTY grabs a bucket from behind the bar and puts it underneath the slow drip. BEV comes downstairs with a fan, plugs it in and points it towards the sofa. MORTY ties a rag around the crack, stopping the drip. BEV continues sopping up water.)

MORTY. I'll call a pipe guy tomorrow.

BEV. A plumber?

MORTY. Yeah, a plumber.

(doorbell rings)

Oh shoot.

BEV. Oh shoot.

MORTY. It's Sam. *(begins to exit)* Oh shoot.

(He stops, comes back, grabs a cowbell which is sitting on the bar. He goes upstairs. BEV is alone looking at the smudged mural. Upstairs we hear MORTY answer the door. BEV goes to the window, opens the curtains and yells into the backyard.)

BEV. Ira, come inside, let me check on you.

(pause)

Ira, do you need to come inside?

(no answer)

Ira…

IRA. *(a voice from outside)* I'm ok.

BEV. Are you sure? Can you check?

(pause)

IRA. I'm ok.

(BEV wipes up more of the water. She walks behind the bar and grabs some more rags. She drops the rags down on the water puddles and steps on them with her heels. She shakes her head at the mess. During this, we have been hearing fragments of the following conversation upstairs.)

JEEP. Hello sir, I'm Jeep Matson.

MORTY. Morty Feinberg. What can I do for ya?

JEEP. Well, as you can see, I'm a photographer, door-to-door actually.

MORTY. Door-to-door photography, huh? Isn't that something.

JEEP. Well it sure is, you know I was just over at –

MORTY. I'm sorry fella... Jeep, is it?

JEEP. That's right, Morty. Jeep. Just like a Jeep.

MORTY. We're having a little...water disaster in the basement at the moment so it's not a terribly good time.

JEEP. Well certainly, sorry to hear that.

MORTY. But sounds interesting. Could you swing on by next time you're in the neighborhood?

JEEP. How does next Tuesday sound.

MORTY. Fine, just fine.

JEEP. Pleasure to meetcha.

MORTY. Enjoy your weekend!

(BEV, mopping up the last of the water on her hands and knees, yells upstairs.)

BEV. Does he like it?

MORTY. Wasn't Sam. It was a salesman.

BEV. Not now!

MORTY. I know, I told him!

(MORTY comes downstairs.)

That was a door-to-door-photographer. You wanna get your picture took on Tuesday?

BEV. My luncheon's ruined.

MORTY. Oh Bevy.

BEV. Everything's going to be damp tomorrow. I'll have to move the girls upstairs. It was going to be so charming down here.

MORTY. I can make the cocktails and bring 'em up on a tray.

BEV. No it's ok, Morty.

MORTY. It'll be like I'm the butler.

*(Squeal of tires and an "oof" from outside. **MORTY** and **BEV** look at each other.)*

Ira.

BEV. Ira!

(They both run upstairs.)

Ira!

MORTY. Ira!

(Sound of front door opening and closing. Muffled chaos. We hear the door open again. The basement is empty. During the following, very subtly, the house seems to settle a little with a low rumble from the earth.)

(from upstairs:)

SAM. No, no, I'm alright, I'm alright.

JEEP. I'm so sorry, I didn't even see –

SAM. These things happen.

BEV. Do you need a hot water bottle Sam?

SAM. No, no.

MORTY. Sit for a moment.

SAM. Alright, that'd be good.

BEV. You can't sit at the table – Cookies on the chairs, cookies on the chairs!

SAM. Op! Cooking a feast, eh?

MORTY. Bev's getting her luncheon together. Let's go downstairs, get you lying down.

BEV. Morty –

MORTY. Bevy, there's no place to sit up here.

SAM. I'm fine, I'm fine.

MORTY. Well I think a little nip will do you good.

SAM. Alright. That I'll take you up on.

JEEP. Here, let me…

(They all come downstairs. **JEEP**, *visibly upset, is helping* **SAM**, *who is wearing the back half of a handmade two-person cow costume. The utters are made of two sets of pink dishwashing gloves sewn onto his belly.)*

SAM. It's all finished, it looks great!

BEV. I apologize. It's a mess, we just had a catastrophe.

JEEP. I'm sorry, Sam.

SAM. Thanks Jeep, I can take it from here. You know, Jeep here took pictures of the whole family today. Color too!

JEEP. And then I tried to kill you tonight.

BEV. Oh you're the photographer.

JEEP. Yes ma'am. Jeep Matson.

BEV. Jeep?

JEEP. Yes ma'am. Jeep. Just like a Jeep.

*(*SAM *starts to sit on the sofa.)*

BEV. Sam, it's wet!

MORTY. Careful.

SAM. Which?

MORTY. The sofa.

SAM. Oh.

JEEP. No, I tell ya, I didn't even see him. He came from behind your shrub and I just backed straight into him.

*(*SAM *goes to sit on the coffee table.)*

BEV. Sam, that's not gonna hold you!

SAM. Oh. Ok.

BEV. Get a folding chair.

(**MORTY** *runs upstairs to grab a folding chair.* **BEV** *continues cleaning.*)

(*to* **JEEP**) Are you the guy with the pony?

JEEP. (*quietly*) No.

(**MORTY** *enters with chair.* **SAM** *sits.*)

SAM. MORTY, this guy is good at his job. Great bed-side manner. No – What do you call that for a picture taker?

JEEP. Oh, just being a good guy, I guess.

SAM. Well, I can't wait to see the photographs. (*looking at the broken pipe*) What happened to your pipe?

MORTY. We're putting a shower in the middle of the room.

SAM. Why? That's gonna get everywhere.

(**BEV** *laughs and shakes her head.*)

MORTY. The roots broke the pipe.

BEV. That's why it's such a mess.

MORTY. It's from the darn willow we just cut down.

SAM. Ah jeepers, that's a pain. How much is that gonna set you back?

MORTY. Sit Jeep, sit.

JEEP. Listen, let me get out of your way here. Sam, here's my card. I know you already have one, but please, take another.

SAM. Ah gee, thanks Jeep.

JEEP. I'm just awful sorry about all this, please, ring me if you find out anything's wrong or –

SAM. Oh, I'm fine, I'll be fine.

JEEP. And your photograph is on me, no arguing, I insist on it. Tuesday. I'll bring it by on Tuesday.

SAM. Listen Jeep…if you insist, I guess my hands are tied. But if that's the case (**SAM** *gets up and walks towards the bar.*) I insist on buying you a drink. Morty, a drink for the photographer.

MORTY. *(whispering to* BEV*)* Get ice!

(BEV *exits.)*

SAM. Put it on my tab.

MORTY. *(in his "bartender voice")* Aw, Sammie, you know yer money's no good here!

SAM. Even better.

MORTY. Jeep, what'll ya have?

JEEP. No, it's out of the question.

SAM. Jeep, I insist on it.

JEEP. Well...

MORTY. Whatever you want. I got everything.

JEEP. Will you fellas join me?

MORTY. Certainly.

SAM. Oh yes.

JEEP. Well, then... I'll have the house special.

MORTY. Water on the rocks and two aspirin, coming right up.

BEV. *(entering with a full ice bucket, shaking her head, laughing at* MORTY*'s dumb joke)* No!

MORTY. No! How about a Street Light?

JEEP. Sounds fine!

(MORTY *starts fixing the drinks.* BEV *continues to straighten up.* JEEP *stands awkwardly, desperately uncertain of what to say and do.)*

This is a nice basement.

BEV. Thank you, we just finished it.

SAM. Ours is similar, but we don't have the knotty pine. Same bar set-up.

MORTY. I just stocked it for Bev's party.

BEV. I'm hosting my first luncheon tomorrow. The Sisterhood, *(explaining to* JEEP*)* the ladies from our Synagogue, are attending. We're new to the neighborhood, and I'm trying to get in.

SAM. I've heard all about it from Gail. She's looking forward to it.

BEV. Well, I've taken a lot of her advice. She's such a good host.

JEEP. Well you see, me doing what I do, I knew you were pretty recent. Last year, this lot was empty, if I remember right.

MORTY. That's right.

BEV. That's right. Excuse me a moment, gentlemen.

(**BEV** *exits upstairs.*)

JEEP. So…what business are you in, Morty?

MORTY. I run a little trophy shop.

JEEP. You don't say!

MORTY. It's called The Trophy Shop. Just moved it here from where we used to be on the South Side.

JEEP. That must be a very in-demand product.

MORTY. Oh yes. It depends on the season of course –

JEEP. Of course.

MORTY. But we do all kinds of things: plaques, medals, medallions, honor statues, you name it. So we keep pretty busy. Starting to do some engraving on personal items as well. Lockets, anniversary plates, pocket knives…

JEEP. Good, good.

SAM. You did great work on those medals for the boys' fishing expedition. Fine work. I tell you, Noah wore his to bed that night. Where did Ira place?

MORTY. Well Sam here, he does the REAL interesting work.

JEEP. Oh, insurance you said, is that right Sam?

MORTY. Is that all he said? Well it is a bit more interesting than *that!*

SAM. Eh.

MORTY. Sam is in the *boat* insurance business.

JEEP. Is that right?

SAM. Always loved boats.

JEEP. Oh yes.

SAM. I get to go out in a lot of 'em. Make a lotta enjoyable trips.

MORTY. Sam, you said you were gonna take me out on the lake this summer.

SAM. I've been busy. The season's sorta dying down now... but... I can ask around.

MORTY. Maybe next summer.

(The phone rings.)

(yelling upstairs) Bev!

BEV. *(yelling downstairs)* Got it!

MORTY. Here's your Street Light. Sit, Jeep.

JEEP. Thank you, Morty.

*(**JEEP** sits at the bar.)*

- - - -

(phone call under dialogue)

BEV. Feinberg residence... Oh hello Mother, I can't talk right now we have guests...yes, I will. Bye.

- - - - -

MORTY. Sam?

SAM. Could I have a Robin Red Breast?

MORTY. Sure.

SAM. Do you know how to make that?

MORTY. Sure do.

*(**MORTY** goes to the bar. He secretly consults his bartending handbook. He begins making the drink. **BEV** comes downstairs. She is carrying a hairdryer. **JEEP** sips his drink.)*

JEEP. Now doesn't that go down smooth!

BEV. It was my mother. I said I'll call back.

SAM. So your luncheon tomorrow…what are you ladies gonna do all afternoon?

(**BEV** *turns on the hair dryer and begins blow drying the sofa. She speaks loudly over the noise.*)

BEV. Just converse and play a little mahjong. I have several courses of goodies.

MORTY. *(yelling over the noise)* Bevy, sweetheart!

BEV. I'm sorry. *(She turns off the hairdryer.)* It's brand new. So, sweets and candies. And… I have a party game up my sleeve.

SAM. A party game? Now we're talking.

BEV. It's rather complicated but very fun. I just read about it…and it's wild. It's called Needle in a Haystack. But it's not actually about needles. It's about pins!

JEEP. I like Bee Pee Bo. Have you played that one?

BEV. Not for a while. Morty adores it.

MORTY. I'm quick. Bev's a genius with riddles though, so it evens out in the end.

BEV. I don't know about that.

SAM. We can *not* play that in my house. Gail and I had a very bad Thanksgiving one year because of Bee Pee Bo.

JEEP. Now, what's the game with the pins?

BEV. Well, everyone gets a handful or so. Safety pins that is. And then you hide them somewhere on you. And then if you cross your leg and someone catches you, you lose a pin. So you win by catching the most pins. But there's more to it than that.

JEEP. Now that sounds fun.

SAM. We should all play.

MORTY. No, it's for ladies.

BEV. No that's a hoot. We should all give it a whirl.

(**MORTY** *gives* **SAM** *his drink. He's made a drink for himself as well.*)

SAM. Thanks Morty.

MORTY. I'll get the pins. They're on the table, sweetheart?

BEV. No those are for the party. The pastels match my motif. But we can use my sewing safeties.

(BEV goes into her sewing basket and counts out pins for everyone.)

SAM. I'm gonna win. I don't cross my leg.

JEEP. Now look at me, I woulda lost a pin if ya caught me.

(SAM and JEEP laugh and cheers their glasses. BEV passes out safety pins.)

BEV. Here ya go. Here ya go. Here. And I think you hide them on you, pinned inside your skirt or jacket…or costume… So no one else knows how many you have left. And then we can add other rules… I guess…oh, I know what would be fun! If you put your drink down. You lose a pin… If someone catches you.

MORTY. Oh, Bevy! That sounds like fun. But we need to get you a drink.

BEV. Oh! Well…alright.

MORTY. *(bartender voice)* What'll ya have sweet-haht?

BEV. Um…oh! Fix me up a Saw Blade.

MORTY. Coming right up.

(He pulls out an orange and a beet and during the following slices them as thinly as possible.)

BEV. This will be fun. A trial run for tomorrow. Did I explain it well enough? Was it clear?

(in unison:)

SAM. Oh yes.

JEEP. Very clear.

MORTY. Very clear.

BEV. Phew.

SAM. Oh Bev, Gail said she wanted me to tell you something.

BEV. Yes?

SAM. Something about the Brownies next Thursday.

BEV. Oh, really?

SAM. What did she say? Time change or actually I have no idea.

(**SAM** *starts wandering around the basement, walking off the limp and checking everything out.*)

JEEP. You lead Brownies?

BEV. No, I'm the helper. It's a wonderful way to meet the ladies in the neighborhood.

SAM. Bev's real helpful, that's what Gail said.

BEV. She did?

SAM. I think so. (*He stops in front of the smeared mural and stares at it.*) Wow, look at this… It's swell.

(**JEEP** *joins him.*)

JEEP. Is it a story?… Are we supposed to piece together something?

MORTY. Nope. Just a scene.

JEEP. Well it certainly is.

MORTY. (*holding out a glass*) Here you are dear.

BEV. As soon as I take my drink…we'll start. Does everyone remember the rules: You're not allowed to cross you leg or put down your drink. And if you do and someone catches you…you lose a pin!

SAM. Should it be legs *and* arms?

(*in unison*)

BEV. Yes!

MORTY. Yes.

JEEP. Oh!

(**BEV** *slowly takes her drink.*)

BEV. Go.

(*Everyone stops talking and watches each other. For a long time.*)

Oh…well… I think the game is supposed to be part of the party. Not stop the party. We just carry on, and chat, and if anyone sees…did I explain it badly?

(in unison)

JEEP. No, no!

SAM. No!

MORTY. Oh no no, we're just going to carry right on. Ah…
Jeep, you listen to the fight last night?

JEEP. No, I was at a wedding.

MORTY. A gig or a guest?

JEEP. As a guest. I strictly stick to the door-to-door work.
Weddings are whole 'nother…

MORTY. I see.

JEEP. Was a buddy of mine. Got married at the Edgewater.

BEV. Oo, very nice.

SAM. So just door-to-door keeps you going?

JEEP. Oh yes. With all the Jewish folks moving in, business
has been real good!

*(**SAM** steps towards **JEEP**, getting very serious.)*

SAM. What, we like getting our picture took more than the
rest?

JEEP. No no, just more people here is all.

SAM. I'm just giving you a hard time.

*(**SAM** laughs, followed by everyone else.)*

JEEP. I follow ya. Say, who won the fight?

MORTY. Sully in 6. Dull fight.

SAM. Sure was.

JEEP. Ah. Well.

(an awkward moment)

MORTY. Photographs.

JEEP. Yes sir!

MORTY. You probably find yourself doing a lot of favors
I imagine.

JEEP. Oh yes, lots of perks for my pals. Everyone wants
a good deal. Too good.

MORTY. I'm the same. I need to mark things up twenty percent 'cause everyone asks for favors...but it makes people feel good. Word of mouth is what makes the business go.

SAM. Bev, I'm going to have to ask you for one of your pins.

BEV. What? *(realizing she's put her drink down)* Oh no!

MORTY. He gotcha, Bevy.

JEEP. Well!

BEV. He sure did. Isn't this a little swell?

JEEP. Sure!

(**BEV** *takes off a pin and presents it to* **SAM**.)

BEV. Here you go. You won this fair and square.

SAM. This is a great game.

JEEP. Sam, I got to ask you a question.

(**SAM** *affixes the pin.*)

SAM. Sure Jeep.

JEEP. Why do you have cow udders on?

MORTY. Oh, that's what he wears daily.

BEV. *(enjoying his joke)* No.

MORTY. No.

BEV. He doesn't really.

SAM. One of the clubs at our temple is having a barnyard square dance tonight with a costume contest.

JEEP. Oh, I see.

SAM. Gail is very competitive and she made these for us.

JEEP. I see.

SAM. It's better when we're in the room together.

JEEP. Ah-ha. I shoulda put that together. Your wife mentioned something about a dance tonight while your boys are camping...oh, well, now I'm REALLY putting it all together. Your boys are here camping I see.

MORTY. Oh, no, that's just our son Ira out there camping by himself. Sam's boys are out on an expedition with the Junior Cherokees Troop.

BEV. Tribe.

MORTY. Tribe.

BEV. Ira's not feeling so well, so he's staying home.

MORTY. But he really wanted to go so he set up camp in the yard.

BEV. I scattered cherries all over the lawn so he can scavenge like a real Indian.

SAM. What a shame. Noah and the little one have been poppin' their tops, ready to go.

JEEP. Oh, well they sure were.

SAM. Sure hope the picture doesn't come out blurry, the boys were roughhousing so much.

JEEP. Oh, I think it'll come out just fine. Your wife looked lovely and the boys looked great in those, whatdaya call 'em – …

SAM. Cherokee headdresses!

JEEP. Well that's right. You have some boys, Sam.

SAM. Oy, they are a handful.

JEEP. They seem like good strong boys. That Noah…

SAM. Sharp as a tack and he can use a knife.

JEEP. Oh, I'll bet! Well I'll tell ya what Sam, the photograph on the sofa, that'll be the one I think.

SAM. Oh?

JEEP. Oh yes, that will be the one.

MORTY. You want to hear something odd?

SAM. Yeah, of course!

MORTY. Well…you know they're putting in all those new phone lines for the new phones that – I don't even know how they're supposed to work – but they're putting them in and apparently there was a three man crew…up working on the lines…they just dropped dead. Fell to the ground. Broad daylight and –

BEV. Well, now, couldn't it be that they just touched the wire and –

MORTY. Dear, these are phone wires, not electrical wires.

BEV. Oh yes, that's right. Well that's just awful.

JEEP. Where was this did you say?

MORTY. Not certain. Someone told me in the shop yesterday.

SAM. In the city I heard.

BEV. Do you know what I heard?

SAM. What?

BEV. This is just terrible, but... Gail was saying, so Sam, I'm sure you know, that the Sterns have been fighting so bad that someone called the police and when the officer showed up they blamed it on the radio show. And their kids both have the driest skin on their faces, had to go to the doctor because the constant crying is causing some sort of irritation. But it's none of my business.

(**BEV** *crosses her leg.*)

SAM. Bev.

BEV. Yes?

SAM. Pin please.

BEV. Oh!

MORTY. Gotcha again, Bevy!

(*blackout*)

(Darkness in the house. A glowing tent is seen in the backyard through the basement window. **IRA**'s *voice is heard.)*

IRA. Those aren't my real parents...but they're wearing my real parents' clothes. They used to say that there was something that lived under the ground that could make things happen. Some bad things that happened happened because of this thing. Things that couldn't be explained. But that was even before people. So who was saying that?... Rah!

Alright. Story time is over Junior Cherokees. Now it's time for...for...the awards. Tonight's award goes to – the award for very Best Brave goes to... Ira!

My fellow braves. I wanted to thank you all for choosing me this evening. I am honored to get this for all my courage and for how fast and strong I am. I will do my best to lead according to the Pledge of the Cherokee. *(He starts to cry.)* It's very fun to be here tonight doing all of these things with you.

(He stops crying. A growl is heard.)

Hello?

- - - - -

(Lights up. Moments later, inside the basement…)

BEV. Oh I don't know them. Wait, are they the people who used to live in Mexico?

SAM. That's right.

BEV. Huh, they brought us that liquor when we moved in.

SAM. He's got a stammer.

BEV. Ah, that's right.

MORTY. Alright, who needs another. *(bartender voice)* Belly on up!

*(**JEEP** stands to go.)*

JEEP. Morty, Bev, thanks for the drink and the hospitality. I should –

MORTY. No Jeep. I'm making you another. And there's nothing you can say about it.

*(**MORTY** takes **JEEP**'s glass.)*

Alright.

*(Everyone gathers around the bar. **BEV**'s about to place her empty glass on the bar, then stops herself.)*

BEV. Oh! Now this could be complicated!

SAM. I suggest a bartending exemption.

JEEP. Fine idea.

(Everyone puts their glasses down on the bar and laughs.)

SAM. Let's see…what do I want? Oh: a Pick-a-dilly!

MORTY. They say for good luck, the second round should always be rum. Everyone game?

JEEP. Fine!

BEV. Sure!

SAM. Well then save the Pick-a-dilly for my third.

MORTY. Rums all around!

SAM. Say Morty, if you want help with fixing that pipe I think I have tools.

BEV. We're calling a plumber.

JEEP. I know a fella.

MORTY. Who?

JEEP. I can find you his telephone number. He's a very good plumber in Rogers Park. Always looking for work.

MORTY. Well thanks, Jeep. I figure we'll see if there's someone local first, and if not, I'll let you know.

JEEP. Sure thing.

BEV. Is gin a beer?

MORTY. What?

BEV. Gin. Is gin a beer? Gin.

(*pause*)

MORTY. What?

BEV. In the movies, when someone drinks a gin...forget it.

SAM. I'm hungry.

(**BEV** *looks at* **MORTY**.)

MORTY. Do you want Bev to fix you something?

BEV. Would you like a nosh?

SAM. Sure. I'll take a sandwich or...what smells so good?

BEV. I was making chopped liver and onions but that's for the luncheon tomorrow.

SAM. Can I taste it?

MORTY. Give him some.

BEV. ... Sure.

(**BEV** *goes upstairs.* **MORTY** *continues to make drinks,* **SAM** *surveys a trophy on a shelf. A momentary lull, then...*)

JEEP. You know a game I used to play as a boy... Grandfather Clock.

SAM. Oh yes!

MORTY. (*yelling upstairs*) Bev, sweetheart! Bring down two potatoes! Large ones. And some twine.

BEV. *(from upstairs)* What?

MORTY. Two potatoes and twine. For –

BEV. Oh boy! We're gonna play Grandfather Clock!?

SAM. Do you play with blindfolds?

MORTY. Not indoors.

JEEP. Morty, there to there? There to there? There to there?

MORTY. There to here.

JEEP. Alright!

(The guys clear things out of the way. **BEV** *comes down with two potatoes and string.)*

BEV. Who will be the first clocks?

SAM. Morty, I challenge you to a round of Grandfather Clock. Do you accept?

MORTY. Tick tock... I accept!

(They all laugh.)

JEEP. All right!

*(***BEV** *hands* **SAM** *and* **MORTY** *potatoes and string.)*

SAM. Uh...truce during preparations?

EVERYONE. Truce!

*(***SAM** *and* **MORTY** *put their glasses on the coffee table and then tie the potatoes to the strings and then tie the strings around their waists.)*

JEEP. I'll make a finish line.

BEV. I can be the referee.

MORTY. Jeep, take two oranges from the bar.

JEEP. Alright!

SAM. Oo boy. I can't believe we're playing Grandfather Clock. You know we called it "Father Time" in my neighborhood.

MORTY. Father Tom?

SAM. Father Time.

(**MORTY** *and* **SAM** *are finished preparing. The potatoes swing between their legs.* **JEEP** *sets the oranges on the floor as* **MORTY** *and* **SAM** *take their positions.* **SAM** *corrects* **JEEP**…)

Oh, starting line *here*.

JEEP. Oh yes!

(**JEEP** *repositions the oranges.*)

SAM. Drinks up.

MORTY. Drinks up!

JEEP. Drinks up!

SAM. Ready.

BEV. Alright, all set?

SAM & MORTY. Yes!

JEEP. Yes!

BEV. 10 o'clock!… 11 o'clock!… MIDNIGHT!

(*The game begins!* **SAM** *and* **MORTY** *laugh and swing their potatoes at the oranges trying to get them to roll across the room.* **JEEP** *and* **BEV** *cheer them on.* **GAIL** *comes down the stairs. She wears the top half of a strangely creepy cow costume. Mask and all. She stands there for a while unnoticed. The game finishes, everyone cheers.* **BEV**'s *face drops as she spots* **GAIL**. *The others turn and see her as well.*)

SAM. Hiya Chicken!… I was coming right back.

GAIL. I've been waiting for over a half an hour…like this. I'm stuck.

(**SAM** *unties a ribbon in the back of the costume and carefully lifts the cow head mask off of his wife.*)

What's the hold-up, Sam?

SAM. I got hit by a car.

GAIL. WHAT?

SAM. It was an accident.

GAIL. Does this mean we're not going to the dance?

MORTY. Nice get up Gail.

JEEP. Hello there Mrs. Fogelberg.

GAIL. Hello. *(to BEV)* Why isn't Ira with the boys?

BEV. He's not feeling well.

GAIL. Oh.

BEV. Gail, may I offer you a drink?

MORTY. Yeah, you want me to fix ya something sweet?

GAIL. No thanks.

BEV. Mine's got no alcohol.

MORTY. Yes it does, sweetie.

BEV. It does? Which one is this?

MORTY. A Tahitian Tease.

BEV. It's so good!

GAIL. Well, what happened? Are you ok?

SAM. It was just a little tap.

JEEP. They have a bush that really blocks the way, I didn't see him.

BEV. *(overlapping with GAIL and SAM)* Morty, we need to take care of that before the party tomorrow.

GAIL. *You* hit him?!

SAM. *He* backed into *me*, it was both our faults.

JEEP. I'm very sorry.

GAIL. Well, can we go?

SAM. I dunno…

GAIL. I'm not going alone…like this…

> *(pause)*
>
> Sam.

SAM. The dance is going all night, Chicken.

GAIL. Sam.

SAM. Chicken.

> *(a heavy pause)*

GAIL. May I have a ginger ale Morty, with a cherry?

MORTY. Big glass or a little glass?

GAIL. Little.

> (**GAIL** *walks to the sofa to sit down.*)

JEEP. Careful Mrs. Fogelberg, the sofa's wet!

BEV. Oh…

GAIL. Well…where would you like me to sit.

MORTY. Would you like to take a seat at the bar, Gail?

BEV. No, no… Hold on, I'll take care of that right away.

> (**BEV** *runs upstairs.*)

GAIL. Jeep, do you get into a lot of accidents?

JEEP. No.

SAM. It was both of our faults sweetheart.

MORTY. *(handing* **GAIL** *her ginger ale, a couple of cherries perched on the top)* Here you are Gail.

> (**MORTY** *knocks on the window.*)

Ira turn off the sprinkler!… On the side of the house…

GAIL. Sam, I'm not staying here.

MORTY. Turn it clockwise…to the right…to the right.

BEV. *(heard from upstairs)* Ira don't play with the sprinkler!

MORTY. *(yelling up)* I told him to turn it off.

BEV. *(from upstairs)* Oh sorry, honey. Sorry, Ira!

> (**BEV** *comes down with a shower curtain and starts spreading it on the sofa.*)

It's Taffallure. It's waterproof. It hasn't been used.

> (**GAIL** *stares at the sofa, then sits uncomfortably on the shower curtain. She puts down her drink.* **SAM** *quietly motions to everyone to let it go. She then crosses her legs and arms. Everyone watches, trying not to laugh… saying nothing.* **GAIL** *notices something's up.*)

GAIL. What?

> (*Everyone breaks into crazy laughter.*)

SAM. *(laughing very hard)* You crossed your arms and leg. And you put down your drink.

GAIL. Ah, I see. The safety pin game.

BEV. *(excited)* Oh, you know it?

GAIL. Yes. We played it at Mrs. Gold's daughter's shower. It was a disaster.

BEV. *(sadly)* Oh.

GAIL. I suppose it's much better as an evening event than a daytime one.

JEEP. Oh yes, we're having fun with it.

BEV. I'll get those snacks.

(**BEV** *slinks upstairs.*)

SAM. Jeep lives over in Evanston.

MORTY. Well, well, well! Is that so?

JEEP. But I actually grew up, oh, about half a mile west of here.

MORTY. How about that?

JEEP. Back when this was still Niles Center.

SAM. A lot of good farmland out here right? That's what our realtor said.

JEEP. That's right, even just five, six years ago that's what it was. But you know this area right here was orchards, mainly. Just trees and trees. Beautiful country. I grew up on one, oh well like I said, just west. Now this place here would have been part of the McCormick's homestead if I'm thinking right. And then what we called town started just back past that.

MORTY. Huh.

SAM. You fish?

JEEP. *Love* to fish.

SAM. What's the biggest fish you caught?

JEEP. Oh, an eight pound walleye. Was a good eating fish.

SAM. Two weeks ago I caught a fifteen pound pike.

JEEP. You don't say!

(**BEV** *enters with a plate of mondel bread.*)

SAM. Ooooo…

GAIL. You ate Sam.

SAM. But it's mondel bread.

GAIL. He used to be very fit when he was in the service.

SAM. *(chewing)* You used to be... I dunno.

GAIL. What?

JEEP. Where'd you serve, Sam?

SAM. I don't talk about it.

JEEP. Alrighty. I understand. Some do, some don't.

MORTY. Where'd you serve, Jeep?

JEEP. Oh, I didn't. I did photographs here in munitions plants and such. I was 4-F.

MORTY. Because of your leg there?

BEV. Morty!

MORTY. Sorry, that was rude of me. None-a-my business.

JEEP. No, that's fine.

MORTY. Alright, I'm gonna make something you'll really like. It's got a frothy top. *(pulling a bowl of eggs out of the icebox)* Because of eggs!

SAM. I do love eggs.

MORTY. Well this one will float *your* boat. Bev, you have any pineapple left?

BEV. Sure, I'll run up and get it.

MORTY. Alright.

(BEV hustles upstairs. MORTY starts making the drink.)

SAM. Esophagus!

GAIL. Huh?

SAM. That's what Noah said he was calling Ira the other day. Some funny joke they have.

MORTY. Is that right?

SAM. All those kids have nicknames. It's code talk right Chicken? Mooka macha racha? You guys speak any languages?

JEEP. No.

MORTY. Nope. Gail?

GAIL. Just Yiddish with my parents.

MORTY. Well yeah, me too.

> (**MORTY** *cracks the egg into the clear shaker. It's very bloody.*)
>
> Op. That's uh… *(Beat. He dumps the egg out, rinses the shaker.)* Would anyone like to select a record while I start over?
>
> (**SAM** *looks through the records.*)

SAM. I wanna learn Brazilian.

MORTY. Jeep. I should set you up with some engraved pens or do-dads for your customers. Whadaya say?

JEEP. Well sure!

MORTY. Now "Jeep." Is that your given name?

JEEP. Nope. Eugene actually.

MORTY. Are most Jeeps Eugenes?

JEEP. Uh, no –

> (**MORTY** *cracks another egg into the shaker. Also bloody.*)

MORTY. Uh… Well…

GAIL. Eggs are bad.

MORTY. How about a round of RaPuPu Sours.

SAM. I like it.

> (**BEV** *comes back down with the pineapple. She's changed out of her wet clothes into a party dress.*)

BEV. Here ya go.

MORTY. Eggs were bad.

BEV. Oh.

MORTY. Gonna fix up some RaPuPu Sours.

BEV. Ooooh. RaPuPu Sours!

> *(blackout)*

(A voice from the tent...)

IRA. I've read about you. Or things like you. All the places you've been. All the things people call you. All the people you've punished. Bubbie told me about how you heard the people in Vilnius who cried for help and she told me I could think about that if I was ever scared or if anyone hurt me. I'm glad you came here.

- - - -

(Lights up. **SAM** *starts a record,* **MORTY** *and* **BEV** *hand out RaPuPu Sours.)*

BEV. Gail, I made the pilgrim hats this week for the Brownies.

GAIL. What?

BEV. You wanted them to have the little felt hats so they could decorate them?

GAIL. Oh, no.

BEV. You had said for Tuesday –

GAIL. They're going to make them themselves.

BEV. Oh. Alright. That'll be fun.

*(**SAM** takes a peppermint from a glass bowl, sniffs it, throws it in the air and catches it with his mouth.)*

GAIL. Don't be such a showoff.

SAM. Say, is Ira signed up for any school clubs?

MORTY. Bev?

BEV. No. We haven't even gotten his teacher's name yet.

GAIL. That'll come at registration. Or no, you'll get it at new student orientation. But there's only one teacher for Noah and Ira's age. Mr. Broder. He's very nice.

BEV. Oh good.

MORTY. Sam, we have to get the boys together again before school starts.

SAM. Noah never wants to play with Ira. I've tried.

GAIL. Ira's too smart for Noah.

BEV. Ira can be very shy.

MORTY. All he does is read.

BEV. That's true. He takes after his Zadie in that. And you know Morty, my father was *also* very small at that age and now he's what, about Jeep's height?

MORTY. Is he? Jeep, stand up.

JEEP. Sure. Sure.

*(**JEEP** stands. They all look at how tall he is.)*

MORTY AND BEV. Yup.

BEV. Yes, about the same.

(**SAM** *starts laughing.*)

SAM. Oh boy...

BEV. What?

SAM. Noah got in trouble for something I thought was pretty clev –

GAIL. It was not nice.

JEEP. What he do?

SAM. So Noah and his buddies have been collecting all these garter snakes from under the new sidewalks. The boys are having a great time and get a bucket full of these little guys and they end up doing a magic show with them in the garage.

GAIL. Not exactly.

SAM. *(laughing)* Well they charged kids a penny to get in... and a nickel to get out! So all the kids are locked in there just screaming their little heads off.

GAIL. Ugh. I'm sorry, we really should get going.

SAM. I just got a new drink.

GAIL. You had us buy all those raffle tickets.

JEEP. What kind of raffle do they have going on over there?

GAIL. A basket raffle.

SAM. A tool basket, sewing odds and ends, candies and sweets.

GAIL. They put a lot of thought into them.

BEV. What a hoot. I'd like to go to that next year, Morty.

GAIL. Thank you so much for –

SAM. They'll call us if we win. That's what the ticket says.

GAIL. But we won't get to *pick* our prize, Sam.

JEEP. Ya know I won my Ford in a contest.

GAIL. Come on Sam.

SAM. Let's finish our nice drinks, Chicken.

(**GAIL** *considers.*)

GAIL. Fine.

BEV. Well that's great!

GAIL. *(picks her half finished drink off of the bar)* Did you say you *won* your car?

JEEP. I sure did. Quite a story.

(Growling sound. Everyone looks at **SAM.***)*

GAIL. Sam!

SAM. I…must be hungry.

MORTY. Bevy, bring us down something else good. I need a nosh too.

BEV. Ok…

GAIL. Sam, you just had a big dinner.

MORTY. Just a little something for us.

BEV. I have some bridge mix and some rugelach in the icebox.

MORTY. Perfect. And maybe some crackers and something salty?

BEV. I have extra dip I can put out…but really, Morty, it's all for the party…

MORTY. Bevy, we're starving.

BEV. Ok.

*(***BEV** *goes upstairs.)*

SAM. Jeep, I'll talk to my pals in the automotive insurance department and they'll work out your car for ya. Cut you a check to take care of the damage.

JEEP. Now Sam, I was certainly at fault here, I don't want you to –

SAM. The car's worse off than me I tell ya. Cracked your taillight I saw… I always did have hard knees.

MORTY. That so?

SAM. Funny thing to say, but yes sir, always did have hard knees. Listen, it'll be fine Jeep. I'll just tell 'em the truth…you were hit by a Holstein!

MORTY. *(laughing)* Well how 'bout that one!

GAIL. Take a photograph.

SAM. Like this?

GAIL. Of the car, Sam. For the guys in automotive.

SAM. Oh! Well that's an idea. Jeep?

JEEP. This is awful nice of you Sam.

(*BEV comes down with snacks.*)

MORTY. Well look at this! Quite a little feast. What do we got here Bevy?

BEV. Chopped egg salad on crackers, herring-apple-d-lite, tiny gefilte fish balls with some chrain and those are just cucumbers on small slices of bread but they're buttered.

SAM. Thanks, Bev.

GAIL. Morty?

MORTY. Yes, Gail.

GAIL. I'm sorry, would you mind putting a little something in this?

MORTY. Of course. (*He tries to choose a liquor bottle.*) Bup, bup, bup.

(*GAIL is sitting at the bar with JEEP. BEV quietly admires her.*)

BEV. Your lips look very nice.

GAIL. It's my color.

BEV. It looks very nice on you.

GAIL. (*quietly*) Tangee's Majesty Red.

(*MORTY tops her off with liquor.*)

MORTY. Here you are, Gail.

GAIL. Thank you, Morty.

(*BEV secretly writes down GAIL's color. Everyone sits quietly.*)

Jeep.

JEEP. Yes Mrs. Fogelberg?

GAIL. Gail.

JEEP. Oh, alright.

GAIL. Your glass is on the bar. I've been looking at it for the last five minutes. No one else noticed.

JEEP. Oh. Look at that. Good eye, Gail.

GAIL. Well…are you going to give me your pin or not?

JEEP. Of course.

(**JEEP** *gives her his pin.* **BEV** *picks up some pins from the table.*)

BEV. Shall I deal you in, Gail?

GAIL. Oh no. I'll win my way in one pin at a time.

(*blackout*)

IRA. *(A voice from the tent…)*

(singing:)

HERE WE ARE, BACK WITH YOU AGAIN.
YES BY-GUM, AND YES BY-GOLLY
KUKLA FRAN AND DEAR OLD OLLIE.
HERE WE ARE AGAIN, HERE WE ARE AGAIN.
HERE WE ARE AGAIN

*(**IRA** laughs a little.)*

Noah says that show is for babies but I still like it sometimes.

Should I sing you another funny song? *(pause)* Ok. And then you can show me the things that will happen next. This is a song that Noah sang last week at Tribe. Mr. Levitch had a talk with him about it after.

*(Then **IRA** sings:)*

THE SQUAW SITS,
ON THE LOG,
SHE DOESN'T WEAR NO CLOTHES.

THE SQUAW SITS,
ON THE LOG,
UP AND DOWN SHE GOES.

OO-OO-OO-OO-OO-OO-OO-OO-OO-OO-OO ALL NIGHT LONG
    SHE SINGS,
OO-OO-OO-OO-OO-OO-OO-OO-OO-OO-OO ALL NIGHT LONG
    SHE SINGS.

THE BRAVE LIES
IN THE LOG –

*(**IRA** stops singing.)*

(speaking) Even though I'm bleeding I'm still a boy. You know that, right?

(loud rumbling into…)

(Lights up in the basement. Everybody's buzzed.)

JEEP. Drinks, drinks, drinks! Who wants drinks and what who wants?

BEV. What?

JEEP. Whadaya want?

SAM. Still working!

GAIL. I'll take another.

BEV. Me too!

JEEP. Alright!

> **(JEEP** *goes behind the bar and pours drinks for the ladies.)*

SAM. Morty. Pin.

MORTY. Ah!

BEV. Hey! Everyone, pick out a swizzle stick. Morty has a whole collection.

MORTY. Take your pick.

GAIL. I collect matchbooks.

BEV. Oh!

JEEP & MORTY. Oh!

MORTY. Oh! Do you know what you should play tomorrow Bevy? Shimmy Shimmy Shoe.

BEV. Isn't that only for four?

MORTY. Right. Hm.

JEEP. So Gail, is this a big collection?

GAIL. Not yet. I'm at twelve. But you see, I'm trying to collect one from every state.

JEEP. Sounds good.

MORTY. Alright! I've got a game to try. Just made this one up on the spot. Oh! You see this up here?

> **(MORTY** *points to a Polynesian mask on the wall.)*

Here's my coconut guy. We like that.

BEV. Yes.

MORTY. So: rules! First, everyone closes their eyes. *(pause)* Everybody, eyes closed!

SAM. Oh, I thought you were still explaining the rules.

MORTY. We can play while I explain.

BEV. Fun!

MORTY. Alright, so everyone's eyes closed?

ALL. Yes.

JEEP. Are yours closed Morty?

MORTY. They sure are Jeep.

JEEP. Alright!

MORTY. Ok. Now. Everyone *QUIETLY*...point to a part of your body.

(Everyone does. Giggles.)

GAIL. Ok.

MORTY. Now quietly put your hands down. And eyes open.

(Everyone opens their eyes.)

Now GUESS!

SAM. Guess what?

MORTY. Guess the body parts!

(Everyone looks around at each other, pondering.)

BEV. My forehead.

(Everyone laughs.)

GAIL. Alright. Beverly, do you know Paper Bag Dramatics?

BEV. No.

SAM. Now we're talking!

GAIL. This is what we used to do at my birthday parties.

JEEP. My sisters used to play this game.

GAIL. It's a well-known game.

SAM. I'm a train conductor!

GAIL. Huh? You don't even know what is in the bag yet or even whose team you are on.

BEV. Are we going to pick teams, Gail?

GAIL. Let's do Morty and me and... Jeep and Bev and... Sam you can judge.

SAM. WHAT?

GAIL. Fine. You can be on our team...they *will* be uneven though.

MORTY. Bev your arms are crossed.

BEV. I'm really terrible at this game.

GAIL. Bev do you have a couple of brown paper bags?

BEV. Sure, plenty.

GAIL. Ok, us girls are going to prepare the bags and then I'll come down, give instructions and we'll play.

BEV. Fun! This is so fun!

(The women walk quickly up the stairs. From here on out when arms are crossed or glasses are put down, people tap each other and exchange pins.)

SAM. Morty, make a man drink for us!

MORTY. Like what?

SAM. I dunno. Brandy or whiskey.

JEEP. I'll have a William Matterstone.

MORTY. I'm not sure what that is.

JEEP. Well, what cordials you have back there?

MORTY. Ah... Crème de Mints or Ments. And a plum thing.

JEEP. Uh... Whatever yer having Sam.

SAM. A belt of brandy.

MORTY. Coming right up.

(MORTY pours three shots of brandy.)

SAM. So. Morty. Who gets what Cherokee awards tonight?

MORTY. Every boy gets something.

SAM. Yeah, but who wins the real one?

MORTY. That's all I can say. Bottom's up!

(The guys down their brandy.)

SAM. But listen to this, they've probably already handed them all out. So there's nothing really...you know. At the very least it's happening right now. Who am I gonna tell? You?

*(**MORTY** looks at **SAM** and smiles.)*

SAM. Jeep, nobody can make this guy talk. Am I right?

JEEP. So it seems, Sam. I'd say that's a good trait in a fella.

MORTY. No. Just the code of the trophy maker.

SAM. Gail heard they're opening a liquor shop over by the chopped steak place.

MORTY. You like that place?

SAM. Yeah, we know the owner. Gail's friends with his wife so we always get the kids a free egg cream or something at the end.

MORTY. Maybe we ordered wrong. I got a stomachache after we ate there.

SAM. You know that's his second wife. His first wife...left him.

MORTY. That's terrible.

JEEP. Geesh.

*(**BEV** and **GAIL** come down the stairs with two large paper bags.)*

GAIL. What's terrible?

BEV. What'd we miss?

SAM. He married one of his waitresses about a month later. The Chops guy I'm talking about.

GAIL. Oh, God. Terrible to poison yourself like that in front of children.

SAM. I didn't go into that but yeah. Real grim. The new wife's real nice to his kids.

GAIL. Ech.

SAM. What?

GAIL. I don't know.

SAM. I thought you liked her?

GAIL. She has a terrible laugh since she got her teeth fixed. There's a whistle. I can't invite her to anything anymore.

SAM. We just had them over!

GAIL. I mean with the Sisterhood when we go out. Jeep, that's the women from our Synagogue. We see shows downtown... Bevy, you'll probably be invited next month.

(**BEV**'s *eyes widen with excitement.*)

Morty, may I use this paper right here?

MORTY. Sure.

GAIL. I swear we were sitting in the audience in the third row and Dorothy's laugh distracted the dancers in the show.

BEV. Ech.

GAIL. Everyone was looking at us. It was very embarrassing.

(**GAIL** *begins to write.*)

JEEP. What did you see?

GAIL. What?

JEEP. What show did you see? I take in shows all the time.

GAIL. A Row Boat For Two.

JEEP. Now what did ya think of that one?

GAIL. Hold on.

(*A pause as* **GAIL** *finishes writing.* **MORTY** *shakes the shaker.*)

Pardon me. I loved the dancing and the Navy scenes.

JEEP. Oh yes. The old guy was good too.

GAIL. He was!

(**GAIL** *puts the written lines of dialog into the bags.*)

Ok, so here are the two bags. Each team gets one. Do we remember our teams?

ALL. Yep.

(*They all move to their respective teams.*)

GAIL. So each team gets a bag. They contain an assortment of things and you have to create a skit using every object in the bag. You *may* use other things in the room. In addition, each bag has a line of dialog to start your scene. Now…you two downstairs. Us three upstairs. Five minutes. Everyone ready?

JEEP. I think so.

GAIL. Ok ready, set… GO!

(**MORTY, GAIL** *and* **SAM** *run upstairs.* **JEEP** *stands awkwardly and* **BEV** *is frantic.*)

BEV. What do we have?

JEEP. Hm?

BEV. What's in our bag? Gail wouldn't let me see what she grabbed. What's in the bag?!

JEEP. Oh! Uh… Grapes…

BEV. Uh huh.

JEEP. A fur thing…

BEV. Ok.

JEEP. And a toy.

(**JEEP** *has taken out grapes, a fur fox neckpiece and a yo-yo.*)

BEV. These are hard. These are very hard. How are we going to make a scene?

JEEP. Who am I? What can I be?

BEV. I don't know!

JEEP. Oh, the line!

BEV. The line!

(**JEEP** *pulls the line of dialog out of the bag. They read it.*)

JEEP. Yeesh!

BEV. Yeesh!

SAM. (*from upstairs*) Fine! Fine!

(**SAM** *runs downstairs.*)

Gail doesn't want me on her team. We got to win. We got to win.

GAIL. *(from upstairs)* Three minutes!

(in unison)

JEEP. Ahhhhhh!

BEV. Ahhhh!

SAM. Ah!

(**SAM** *pulls the shower curtain off the sofa.* **JEEP** *and* **BEV** *run around the room.*)

(blackout)

(**IRA**'s *voice from the tent glowing in the window…*)

How is this night going to be different from all other nights? The roots grow. The leak. Jeep hits the man with his car. The cow arrives. My scab tears and bleeds. The grown-ups play and dance. The first born cries. Then the phone call. Then the lightning strikes the tents. And they will *all* burn. Just like you promise.

(Lights up. **BEV,** **SAM** *and* **JEEP** *are hiding.)*

SAM. *(yelling upstairs)* Who's gonna go first?

MORTY. Well once we come down you are gonna see what ours is about.

JEEP. But when you see us you're gonna know what ours is about!

GAIL. We'll come down, but everyone try not to really look at each other. Ready or not, we're coming down.

(in unison)

SAM. Ok!

JEEP. Alrighty.

BEV. Ok!

SAM. Wait. Should we turn off the lights?

MORTY. Yes.

*(****MORTY****'s hand appears around the corner and he flips the switch on the wall.* **MORTY** *and* **GAIL** *come down slowly, keeping their heads down.* **MORTY** *has a mop on his head, ladies' makeup and a bathroom towel shawl,* **GAIL** *has a comb mustache attached to her face.* **SAM** *is wearing the shower curtain from the sofa like a Greek robe and shower curtain ring earrings, lipstick and is maybe Cleopatra.* **JEEP** *has the paper bag on his head.* **BEV** *is a lamp with a shade on her head and the yo-yo as the pull string.)*

GAIL. Who is going to go first?

BEV. We will.

MORTY. Can we look?

SAM. Wait. We need to get into position.

BEV. You can turn on the light when we're ready.

MORTY. Alright.

*(****BEV, SAM*** *and* ***JEEP*** *get into position.)*

BEV. Ok Morty, you can turn on the light.

MORTY. Alright.

*(****MORTY*** *turns on the light.)*

(**SAM** *lounges across the bar stools.* **BEV** *and* **JEEP** *stand nearby.*)

JEEP. *(singing)*
CLEOPATRA WAS A LADY
FROM THE RIVER NILE.
HERE'S A LAMP –

(**SAM** *pulls* **BEV***'s lamp string.*)

BEV. On.

JEEP. *(singing)*
– TO LIGHT HER WAY.

SAM. *(singing)*
AND A BAG TO COVER JEEP'S SMILE.

(**GAIL** *and* **MORTY** *laugh and clap enthusiastically.*)

MORTY. Looking good Sam!

GAIL. Who thought of the song?

BEV. Jeep did.

(**JEEP** *raises his hand.*)

GAIL. That's excellent, Jeep.

JEEP. *(quite pleased)* Thank you.

GAIL. Everyone was very good. Shall we Morty?

MORTY. Ours is a song too!

BEV. Oo!

(**SAM** *and* **JEEP** *cross and sit on the couch as* **GAIL** *and* **MORTY** *prepare their performance.* **BEV** *sits on the floor in front of coffee table.*)

JEEP. Sofa's still wet.

(**GAIL** *and* **MORTY** *turn and start their show. Singing:*)

GAIL.
THERE WAS AN OLD MAN FROM LONDON,

MORTY.
WHO LOVED AN OLD LADY CURMUDGEON.

GAIL.
HE BOUGHT HER FINE CLOTHES AND CHOP SUEY, BUT
WHEN HE GOT FRESH SHE SAID:

MORTY.
>   "OH PHOOEY! ON YOU-IE! WHY DON'T YOU GO BACK TO ST. LOUIE!"

BOTH. *(in "harmony")*
>   THEEEEEE ENNNNNND.

>   *(BEV, JEEP and SAM clap.)*

BEV. Good one Morty!

JEEP. Gail, ya got good rhythm!

SAM. If I was still the judge, you'd win.

GAIL. Morty, may I borrow a trophy?

MORTY. Sure.

>   *(MORTY hands GAIL a trophy from behind the bar. She smiles, looks at SAM, and walks toward him as she says…)*

GAIL. I am honored to present this trophy to the most handsome and sweet… *(She turns to BEV.)* LAMP I have ever seen!

>   *(BEV screams with surprise and excitement. Everyone laughs.)*

BEV. Ahhhhhhhhhh!

SAM. Oh!

>   *(BEV finds another trophy in the room…)*

BEV. And this is for Gail, for her wonderful performance and for being my new friend and so dear!

GAIL. Thank you Bev.

>   *(SAM looks at GAIL's trophy.)*

SAM. Let's see it. *(reading the trophy inscription)* "Best Browler."

MORTY. These are my samples and seconds.

BEV. Oh! There's that game where, oh no, is this too many games? Can we do another game? Is this too many games?

EVERYONE. No!

BEV. *(laughing)* Do you know what we should do? The one where everyone writes down a dance –

MORTY. Oh yes!

BEV. – and then they pull from the hat. Jeep do you mind?

JEEP. No!

BEV. Then we play a song, someone draws from the hat, and we try to call out their dance.

MORTY. But keep it simple. Nothing too fancy.

BEV. But that makes it fun Morty!

MORTY. You're right Bev.

(BEV and MORTY hand out paper and pencils.)

BEV. Write down a dance, everyone write down a dance.

JEEP. Well I'll say this: us guys don't know as many dances as you ladies.

SAM. Speak for yourself. I can cut a rug.

MORTY. I'll pick out a song.

BEV. Now is everyone writing down a dance?

(MORTY goes to the record player to pick out a record. Everyone else writes.)

Jeep, would you like to go first?

MORTY. No, someone who has played before should go first.

BEV. Ok, I'll go.

(She pulls a piece of paper from JEEP's hat, looks at it and smiles. MORTY pulls out a record and places it on to the record player.)

BEV. Pick something upbeat. No pick something slow. I don't want to give it away so easy.

MORTY. I think I picked good.

(Music starts. BEV smiles big and starts to do the Charleston very slowly to the sappy song. Everyone watches intently.)

JEEP. Waltz!

SAM. What!?

JEEP. I don't know.

GAIL. Charleston for Pete's sake!

(*They all cheer.*)

MORTY. Now you pick out a dance, Bev's gonna keep dancing and we try to guess your dance.

SAM. Ok.

(**BEV** *keeps doing the Charleston.* **GAIL** *picks a song out of* **JEEP**'s *hat, and starts doing a more upbeat dance.*)

JEEP. Waltz!

SAM. Lindy Hop!

GAIL. Yes!

(*They all cheer and laugh.* **BEV** *and* **GAIL** *keep dancing.* **SAM** *picks out of the hat, reads the slip of paper.*)

SAM. Uh oh. Jeep?

JEEP. Waltz?

SAM. Yes!

JEEP. I wrote that one!

(*More cheers. The party is in a wonderful frenzy.*)

MORTY. Now it's your turn, you pick one, and from here on out it gets very complicated.

(**SAM, GAIL** *and* **BEV** *are all doing their separate dances at the same time while the music plays.* **JEEP** *picks a dance out of the hat, reads the paper, frozen.*)

JEEP. Oh! Aaah! Ahhhhhhhhhhh! Aaaaaaaaaaoooooooh! Aaaaaa…

GAIL. (*bailing out* **JEEP**) Let's have another drink!

ALL. Yeah!

(**MORTY** *goes to make drinks,* **SAM** *and* **GAIL** *go to sit on the couch together. That game is over, but the party is still in full swing.*)

BEV. (*to* **JEEP**) Are you *sure* you never use a pony?

JEEP. I never use a pony.

BEV. Ok, well, someone has been going around with a pony. Mrs. Leiber said she saw it last week.

JEEP. It's this new guy from way west of here. If I lose another sitting to that guy with – Ya know, he is not even a registered photographer. And his pictures are amateur.

GAIL. I heard he lets the thing go all over the place.

SAM. That's why we didn't use him.

JEEP. I've heard lots of complaints about that thing tearing up yards.

BEV. I bet the kids love it though.

GAIL. I think it's distasteful. To pose with an animal.

SAM. Eh.

BEV. I like it here. The insects and animals. All the space. Am I talking too much? It's better here. The South Side had –

MORTY. Bevy.

BEV. It was kind of all of the sudden, it was time to move. Right Morty? It got to be too much. I think kids nowadays, they just don't –

MORTY. Bevy, not now.

BEV. When Ira's older he'll start to fit in. That's what happens with kids.

MORTY. I was a strange looking kid. But Bev always was a looker.

BEV. Morty!

JEEP. I think it's a great place for kids to grow up. Real safe. Quiet. About twenty years ago we had some gangster trouble but really not much since.

BEV. Jeep, sit.

SAM. What kind of trouble?

JEEP. Oh just run-of-the-mill gangster trouble. There was a chase where two Bureau fellas got shot.

MORTY. Bev's father made two-way glass for Capone.

BEV. Morty.

MORTY. What? It's a good story.

BEV. I don't like talking about it. I don't like to brag.

MORTY. Her father is a glassmaker. Cuts custom glass.

BEV. Well not anymore. This is when I was little. I would get to go with him sometimes in my nightgown with my sister and we would ride in his buggy...isn't that funny how times have changed...anyway he dropped off two-way glass for some of the old time Italian mobsters. I didn't realize it at the time but it was them.

GAIL. That is much more exciting than my parents. They did accounting and taxes.

SAM. FOR THE MOB!

(*They all laugh.*)

GAIL. Stop it. No not for the mob.

MORTY. Jeep, tell us about your girl.

BEV. Oh, yes!

GAIL. You have a girl? What's her name?

JEEP. Oh. I don't have a girl.

(*a pause*)

BEV. Let's dance! Would you like to put something else on? You can borrow a dress. My yellow one you like.

GAIL. No, thank you Bev. I'm comfortable.

BEV. Are you sure? We can go upstairs and pick something out for you.

GAIL. No, I'm fine.

(**MORTY**, **SAM** *and* **JEEP** *sit and drink slowly, watching the women dance.*)

MORTY. Jeep.

(**MORTY** *whispers something to* **JEEP**. **JEEP** *smiles, nods and slyly exits.*)

SAM. What?

(**MORTY** *whispers to* **SAM**. **SAM** *smiles.*)

That's smart thinkin'. (*sudden idea*) Oh! Hey Jeep!

(**SAM** *runs up the stairs after* **JEEP**. **MORTY** *drinks. The women dance for a while.*)

GAIL. I'm smoked!

(**GAIL** *admires* **BEV**'s *dance move.*)

How do you do that?

BEV. This? I don't know?

GAIL. It's good.

(*beat*)

BEV. I make an eight.

(*They both do the move. The upstairs door opens, and* **SAM** *yells down.*)

SAM. Where's the garage light?

MORTY. (*yelling*) Hold on!

(**MORTY** *goes upstairs. The women dance.* **BEV** *glances out the window.*)

GAIL. Something's odd about him.

BEV. What do you mean?

GAIL. Well, not odd. He is just sort of strange. Quiet. You know.

(**BEV** *stops dancing.*)

BEV. He'll grow out of it.

GAIL. Jeep, Bev.

BEV. Oh. I guess so. He seems nice.

(**BEV** *starts dancing again.*)

GAIL. Maybe he's just shy. You know he was very good with my boys. Had them laughing at his jokes. Couldn't get them to sit still but...

BEV. What did you wear?

GAIL. I put Sam in his good suit. And I wore my green taffeta dress. With the feather boning.

BEV. That sounds lovely. Maybe we should get a sitting. I took Ira to Marshall Fields when he was a toddler but… I think that would be nice to have a photograph for my parents now that they don't see him everyday.

GAIL. You're very thoughtful.

BEV. *(truly touched)* Thank you Gail.

GAIL: I'm smoked!

BEV. Gail, don't mention this to Morty, but Ira's not sick. He keeps hurting himself. Yesterday it was something very bad.

GAIL. How did he hurt himself?

*(**MORTY** comes back downstairs.)*

MORTY. Hiya ladies.

BEV. Hiya.

*(**MORTY** tries to do the "eight move" for a moment.)*

MORTY. I can't do it.

*(**SAM** and **JEEP** come down the stairs with a camera.)*

JEEP. It's not a snapshot camera, but it'll work!

*(Everyone cheers. **GAIL** fixes her hair and pretends to not be excited. **BEV** beams.)*

GAIL. Oh, here we go.

MORTY. Ladies, do the Mambo!

*(**BEV** and **GAIL** do the Mambo.)*

JEEP. Beverly, Gail would ya mind stopping for a moment so I can get a picture of you dancing?

(Both women freeze mid dance. Big smiles.)

SAM. The girls dancing, that's a good photo. I'll take one of those. Gail!

*(**SAM** holds up his thumb.)*

JEEP. Get in a little closer.

(They scoot in.)

Swell. Very nice, ladies. 3, 2, 1.

(The camera flashes. The phone rings upstairs.)

BEV. It's so late.

MORTY. I better get it.

(**MORTY** *goes upstairs.* **BEV** *turns the music down.*)

GAIL. I worked a week on the head alone. And only you three saw it, you *four* saw it. That's fine, we'll save it for something.

JEEP. You two could be Mrs. O'Leary's cow for Halloween.

GAIL. That's right!

- - - -

(*overlaps*)

MORTY. Feinberg residence...yes it is...well hello sir... well that's a funny thing. He's here... Yes sir...just a moment.

- - - -

(**MORTY** *comes downstairs.*)

It's for you, Sam.

GAIL. What?

MORTY. It's Mr. Levitch, nothing to – everything sounds fine. It's a funny thing, he meant to call you but he called me.

BEV. Fogelberg, Feinberg.

SAM. They have telephones at campgrounds now?

(**GAIL** *looks at* **SAM.**)

SAM. I'm sure it's fine, Chicken.

(**SAM** *goes upstairs.*)

JEEP. Who's that?

MORTY. The tribe leader.

GAIL. Boys probably got into some trouble.

BEV. I'm sure everything's fine.

- - - -

(*Phone conversation upstairs. Happens under the downstairs conversation.*)

SAM. Hello...this is he...oh...may I speak to him?... No,
I understand... Really? Well I-...uh-huh... Yes...yes,
thank you...thank you, I'll talk to my wife and then-...
thank you... Bye.

- - - -

(**SAM** *comes down.*)

BEV. Is everything alright?

SAM. Noah's crying and wants to come home.

GAIL. What?

SAM. They said he won't stop crying.

GAIL. Noah?... We should go get him and the little one.

SAM. He'll be fine. Kids are fine. He'll be fine.

GAIL. Sam, he's scared?

SAM. He'll be fine.

GAIL. It's now or in the middle of the night... Is that a can
of peanuts?

(**GAIL** *points to a can on the shelf.*)

BEV. No, it's a joke.

GAIL. Oh.

SAM. Call Mrs. Hesselstein and see if she's picking up her
son...she said she didn't want him there the whole
night.

GAIL. Oh that's a thought...may I use your telephone?

MORTY. Certainly.

GAIL. You call.

SAM. Gail just call her. She hates me.

GAIL. Oh yes...she does.

(**GAIL** *goes upstairs to use the phone.* **MORTY** *goes to the
mural.*)

(*yelling from upstairs*) Oh! Switch off the record player!

(**MORTY** *turns off the record player.*)

- - - -

(from upstairs we hear...)

Hi, Mrs. Hesselstein...sorry to phone so late...
Gail... Gail Fogelberg... I'm not feeling well and was
wondering if you're picking up Joshua tonight. Oh
alright, I see.... No, no, no I was looking for someone
to pick up my boys... I understand...sorry to bother...
thank you.

- - - -

*(**SAM** is laughing to himself. **MORTY** makes his way over
to him.)*

MORTY. What?

SAM. You know, when I was in the service, there was this
joker we called Gums. And this fella, he was from, I
don't remember where he was from now, the South or
West I guess, but he –

MORTY. Guns?

SAM. Yeah, Gums. And this fella –

JEEP. Morty, may I get another nip of just the rum on ice...
stomach's a little off.

MORTY. Sure thing.

*(**MORTY** goes back to the bar to make **JEEP** the drink.)*

You need a, uh – Alka-Seltzer?

JEEP. No, no, just the rum should do 'er.

BEV. *(not hearing **MORTY**'s offer)* You want a Alka-Seltzer?

JEEP. No, no, just the rum should do'er.

*(**GAIL** comes back downstairs.)*

GAIL. They already picked up Joshua.

SAM. They'll be fine.

GAIL. I know.

*(Everyone sits quietly. **MORTY** looks at the mural.)*

MORTY. In the morning I'm going to fix this, Bevy.

BEV. Ok.

MORTY. I think I can do it.

BEV. Ok.

GAIL. *(smiling a bit)* You can put the music back on.

BEV. Can I pick?

MORTY. Sure, sweetheart.

(**BEV** *finds a record.*)

SAM. Good party.

(in unison)

JEEP. Oh yes.

GAIL. Yes.

(**MORTY** *and* **BEV** *smile at each other. She puts on a record.*)

MORTY. I thought you said "Guns" but it was "Gums".

SAM. "Gums".

(**SAM** *kisses* **GAIL** *and she smiles.* **MORTY** *and* **BEV** *get closer. They start to dance.* **JEEP** *goes over to make another drink. He downs it, turns and watches the couples dance.* **MORTY** *dips* **BEV.** *After a little while…*)

JEEP. Alrighty. It's late. I'm gonna hit the road.

(The couples stop dancing.)

BEV. Lovely meeting you, Jeep.

MORTY. Yessir!

SAM. Jeep-Jeep! Hope to see ya soon.

JEEP. Well, Tuesday, isn't that so? I'll drop you off your *complimentary* portrait on Tuesday.

SAM. That's right.

GAIL. If it's after dinner, we can all have a cocktail in *our* basement.

JEEP. That sounds fine. Thanks for everything!

MORTY. You're welcome, Eugene!

JEEP. Bye now.

(**JEEP** *walks up the stairs.*)

MORTY. Nice guy, huh?

Night cap?

ALL. Yeah.

(**MORTY** *makes drinks.*)

SAM. Oh! Morty! D'ya got that kooky record I borrowed you?

MORTY. Oh…over there.

(**SAM** *digs through the records, humming a kooky song to himself. He pulls a record out and excitedly holds it over his head. He puts it on. It's something vaguely Polynesian, playful but goofy.* **GAIL** *sits on the edge of the sofa, eating snacks.* **SAM**, **MORTY** *and* **BEV** *sit by the bar, hazily listening to the record.*)

SAM. It's nice to have a house of your own, right Morty?

MORTY. That's right Sam. Let's do another game!

SAM. Stretch!

GAIL. Sam!

SAM. What?

GAIL. *(lighter)* A pocket knife game? Inside?

BEV. Musical chairs! No I'm too sleepy.

GAIL. Do you play golf, Bevy? You should come play with the girls and me.

BEV. Certainly. I can learn.

GAIL. I'll bring you a club. We can practice in my yard.

MORTY. We did this spoof in the service where we all put our shoes on the wrong feet and then we'd –

SAM. *(chanting)* I'm Private Wrongshoe how do you do?

SAM & MORTY.

WHEN FOLKS SEE MY TRACKS THEY HAVE A HEART ATTACK.

WHEN I BOOGIE WITH JILL IT GIVES HER A THRILL.

WHEN I WALK INTO FLORSHEIM THEY HOLLER "CLOSING TIME!"

(*They laugh and sloppily hug.*)

SAM. Next summer, we'll boat all summer long. How's that sound?

MORTY. Yessir. Oh boy, I'm gonna sit.

SAM. Yep.

MORTY. Oo!

(**SAM** *crosses to* **BEV**.)

SAM. I sure liked those finger foods you made! What's –

BEV. My herring-apple-d-lite.

SAM. No, that dip? What was that swell dip?

BEV. The pink one?

SAM. Nope, that one was a little too goofy for my taste... the other.

MORTY. Oh, Hollywood Glaze. It's a classic. It's gonna be a hit at your luncheon tomorrow.

(*beat*)

SAM. Good night.

MORTY. Good night.

(*They listen to the record.*)

SAM. Left, left –

(**MORTY** *joins in the military march chant.*)

MORTY & SAM. I left my wife and children in the kitchen in a starving condition without any gingerbread left, left (*repeat*)...

(**SAM** *is marching in place and starts marching out of the room.* **MORTY** *gets up and marches with him.*)

MORTY. When did we stop watching safety pins?

(*They march up the stairs.*)

GAIL. Bevy...

BEV. Yes?

(*We can hear the men chanting upstairs, tromping through the house...*)

GAIL. Bevy I – ... I don't think Ira hurt himself.

BEV. What?

GAIL. I think that it might have been my boys. That hurt him.

(beat)

BEV. What?

GAIL. The little one told me that something happened.

BEV. It was your boys that did that to him?

GAIL. Yes.

BEV. No, Gail.

GAIL. I'm sorry Bev. I'll talk to Sam. He'll make sure the boys take it easier on Ira.

BEV. Gail, I had to put him in a Kotex.

GAIL. What?

BEV. He bled through his pants.

(BEV gets up and looks out the window. GAIL is frozen. The men re-enter, marching and chanting, unaware.)

GAIL. Sam!

(The men stop.)

SAM. How much did ya pay for your house?

GAIL. Sam.

SAM. What? We're friends! I wanna know what they are going for now.

MORTY. Fourteen five.

SAM. That's not bad.

(loud crack of thunder)

SAM. Golly!

GAIL. I wanna go home.

SAM. Alright, alright.

BEV. Morty, I'm going to go check on Ira.

MORTY. No, I got it.

(MORTY goes to the window.)

Kiddo! How are ya kiddo?

IRA. *(voice from outside)* I'm ok.

MORTY. Good. He's good.

GAIL. I can come over early tomorrow to help set up your luncheon. 9 o'clock? Or should I come earlier?

BEV. Thanks, Gail.

GAIL. It's gonna be a lovely party.

(Flash of lightning. Very loud thunder. The lights go out.)

(Then…the stage changes.)

*(We are now outside in the backyard. The tent is in the foreground. Next to it, a weeping willow stump. Below, the sod is black earth and further down a dark, swirling cavern of roots. Behind, we see the back of the house and the ground level window looking into the basement. In the tent, **IRA** sits up on his knees. We see him silhouetted by the light of a camping lantern. He wears an Indian headdress. The sprinkler is on, we can hear it quietly watering the lawn.)*

IRA. Hello?

*(**IRA** prepares to exit the tent, grabs a trophy he has in the tent with him, and quickly rushes through the flaps of the tent. He's barefoot, in pajamas. He is small for a nine-year-old. Pale and very delicate. He peers into the darkness, trophy at-the-ready, tense. From inside the house we hear…)*

BEV. 10 o'clock!… 11 o'clock!… MIDNIGHT!

(The adults play Grandfather Clock inside, as before, cheering and hollering until it subsides.)

SAM. Hiya Chicken!

*(**IRA** looks at the window, the giant cow head is illuminated. It's the same as before, but now more strange. As **IRA** looks away the light in the window fades. He walks gingerly to the stump and places the trophy behind it. He stands beside the stump. He is in physical pain, but he pushes through it.)*

IRA. Ok. Stand and recite the Pledge of the Cherokee. Hands on your hearts. *(He places his hand on his heart.)* I will honor my tribe, my leader, my brothers, my huntsman.

(He stretches his arms out then sweeps them in a circle.)

I will be brave and lead when told to lead and lift when told to lift.

(He lifts his arms to the sky.)

Honor and strength is inside and out.

(Action of shooting a bow and arrow.)

Turn to the left, turn to the right, we the boys who read the paths from the star's great light.

Hip Hip Ty Ty *(clap).*

(IRA winces in pain. The roots respond, growing underneath IRA. He feels them rumble. We see MORTY at the window.)

MORTY. Ira turn off the sprinkler!

(IRA is startled. He walks to the sprinkler.)

…On the side of the house…

(IRA walks to the spigot.)

Turn it clockwise…to the right…to the right.

BEV. *(heard from upstairs)* Ira don't play with the sprinkler!

MORTY. *(yelling up)* I told him to turn it off.

BEV. *(from upstairs)* Oh sorry, honey. Sorry, Ira!

(Lights fade in the window. IRA sits in the grass. From inside the house we hear a roar of laughter. After a moment IRA suddenly growls in anger. He turns and looks at the stump. He looks around to make sure no one is watching. He talks to the stump.)

IRA. Yesterday I was hiding from Noah. I went in the alley behind here and made boats out of cans to float in the puddles. Noah and his brother found me and said they wanted to play. Which sounds fun, but it's not. They threw rocks. They broke my boats. Other boys came. Noah took out his pocket knife and said let's play stretch. (**IRA** *gets very quiet for a while.*) It's not better here. It's worse.

(*The spirit "arrives" in the tent: roots moves, tent glows.*)

I've read about you. Or things like you. All the places you've been. All the things people call you. All the people you've punished. Bubbie told me about how you heard the people in Vilnius who cried for help and she told me I could think about that if I was ever scared or if anyone hurt me. I'm glad you came here.

(**IRA** *goes to the tent, peeks through the flaps, then enters. He is overtaken by visions. The sounds of this night and the future are faintly heard.*)

I can see the Glaciers. I can see the buffalo. And the Chickasaw. The trees being planted. The sidewalks being poured. (*beat*) How is this night going to be different from all other nights?

(*A camera flash by the side of the house. We hear:*)

SAM. Let's do one with me. Like it happened. Hey, who am I… "Oof!"

JEEP. You?

(*camera flash*)

SAM. Get a photograph of the taillight. They'll need to see the crack.

JEEP. Okay…got it.

SAM. I can take one if you like. Of you and the car.

JEEP. I don't need to be in a picture. And it's pretty complex.

SAM. Sure.

JEEP. Is there a way to have a bit more light?

SAM. Sure. Morty! Where's the garage light!

(**IRA** *is in silhouette in the tent.*)

IRA. I see Jeep as a weak little boy. His sisters pick him up and carry him behind the barn. They're holding him down. The tall one takes the braces off his legs. They put him in the bucket and lower him down into the well. "Eugene in the ground, oh so deep, down in the well where the spiders creep." And now it's night. "Pull me out!" But they're gone. "Nellie? Myrtle? Alma?" They're inside. Laughing at him. And in the dark he cries. And then...he stops. Because there you are. And you make the rain come. And the water rises and rises and carries Eugene's tiny body right up out of there.

In the morning his sisters make him promise not to tell on them. And then a hornet stings Alma on the lip and Myrtle on the nose and Nellie on the eye. And as they scream and scream, Jeep walks out and whispers down into the well, "goodbye." And "thank you." And you liked that.

(The roots grow and move underneath the tent.)

Then he grew up strong and became a man. I see... he's here tonight...because he needs to take pictures of everything that happens. Noah and his family on the sofa. The tail light. The mothers dancing. Me.

(JEEP is suddenly standing by the tent.)

JEEP. Ira?

(No answer. JEEP turns to leave.)

IRA. Hi, I'm Ira.

JEEP. Hello there. I'm Jeep.

IRA. Like from the cartoon.

JEEP. That's right!

(quiet)

Are you having a fun time out here?

IRA. Sure.

JEEP. You're feeling a little under the weather your parents said?

IRA. I'm feeling better tonight. And I know tomorrow will be good.

JEEP. Well there's a bit of a cool nip there in the air, so just seeing if you're doing alright out here.

IRA. You hit someone.

JEEP. Pardon?

IRA. You hit someone.

(**JEEP** *sits down on the stump. He picks up the trophy.*)

JEEP. Oh, yes. I sure did. Just a bump. It was a close call. You having –

IRA. Noah's dad.

JEEP. Yup.

IRA. How did you win your car?

JEEP. Guessing bolts in a jar. Always been good with eyeing things like that.

IRA. Me too.

JEEP. The trick is counting a corner and then multiplying it by how many of those you think make up the jar. Pretty neat. I guessed it on the dot.

IRA. I learned six things from the Cherokee handbook tonight.

JEEP. Oh, did ya?

IRA. Leaves of three let it be; berries white, poisonous sight. That's pretty important. And then mainly about identifying things: I learned some new animal tracks. Most people don't know those. Which is good. I learned some new birds. Different kinds of clouds. State flags. I learned that deer antlers can grow more than an inch a day.

JEEP. How bout that.

IRA. That's the fastest growing animal thing we know about. *(a pause)* You're supposed to take my picture, Jeep.

JEEP. Well sure. You want me to take your picture?

IRA. Ok.

JEEP. You wanna come out?

IRA. No.

JEEP. Ok...that's all right I'll just get you in the tent. I'll set up.

(**JEEP** *puts the trophy in front of the tent, sits on the grass and opens his camera case.*)

Do you know where Missouri is?

IRA. Yes.

JEEP. When I was a boy *I* liked to go camping. We'd visit my uncle in Missouri. He'd take my sisters and me down to a little place called Agate Lake and we'd, well we'd fish, and cook outside, and make lean-tos out of sticks. And then when I was twelve or thirteen...do you know what a quarry is?

IRA. Yes.

JEEP. They took sand from the quarry there and they built a real nice swimming beach. I had polio when I was much younger, but swimming was always something I could do. Always loved the water.

IRA. Do you remember seeing the buffalo?

JEEP. Oh no. That was before my time. But there used to be farms right here when I was your age.

IRA. When I was a boy I liked to go camping too.

JEEP. Alright. All set. You wanna open the tent?

(**IRA** *opens the tent flaps.* **JEEP** *hands the trophy to* **IRA** *through the flaps.*)

IRA. I didn't really win this trophy. I just pretend that. My dad made it for me.

JEEP. Pretty neat. Alright. Now, hold the lantern up. Good. Now, there's gonna be a flash, ok?

IRA. Ok.

JEEP. Three, two, one..

(*flash*)

Gonna be a good one, Ira.

IRA. And now take a picture of the lightning.

JEEP. Oh… Well, now that's something I don't think I can actually –

IRA. I'm just joking.

(Faint heat lightning far away. There's a hint of movement deep inside the root cave.)

JEEP. Well, Ira, you were a fine subject. Ira the Indian, I'm off. Have a good camp out kiddo ok?

IRA. Ok.

JEEP. Alrighty. Bye now.

IRA. Bye.

(JEEP leaves.)

(IRA is all alone. He comes out of the tent and perches on the stump.)

Next month is my birthday. But nobody will be coming to celebrate. There won't be any parties here for a while. All of the boys –

(The lights come on in the window.)

MORTY. Kiddo! How are ya kiddo?

IRA. I'm ok.

MORTY. Good. He's good.

(MORTY walks away.)

All of the boys are out camping and they're not coming back. School starts in a week and my class will be much smaller than they thought because of the things that are about to happen…right…

GAIL. *(offstage)* It's going to be a lovely party.

IRA. … Now.

(Flash of lightning. Loud thunder. The inside lights flicker off. The crickets return.)

On Tuesday Jeep will deliver a family portrait. But Gail and Sam will be sad. And everyone else too. Because those blurry boys are gone.

The alleys will be quiet now. No one but me. It will be like that for a while.

And I saw what will happen after that. I will have a brother. Isaac. And that's his right name. We'll have a lot of fun playing games that I teach him. He'll think my stories are very funny.

The End

SPECIAL THANKS

Sue Kessler, Noel Joseph Allain, Jay Maury, Maria Portman Kelly, William Burke, John Budge, Paul Davis, Sarah Swafford, James Hunting, John Czop, Doug Wright, David Clement, Annie Baker, Goldie Goldblum, Charlene Bos, Polly Carl, David Dower, Jenny Gersten, Lisa Steindler, Mark Russell, Meiyin Wang, Andrew Kircher, Quita Sullivan, Rabbi Lehrfield, Di Glazer, Mark Subias, Mark Armstrong, Casimir Nozkowski, Jon Knust, Nicholas Moreno, Shelley Miles, Ars Nova, Six Point Brewery, Acme Fish, Vineyard Arts Project, Maria Striar, Adam Greenfield, Lisa Joyce, Leah Walton, Tim Chawaga, Rebecca Guber, Marge Betley, Sarah Lazarus, Anna Elliot, Cynthia Flowers, Hanna Cheek, New York Theatre Workshop, Maggie Buchwald, Brian Mullan, Jason Eagan, Emily Shooltz, Jeremy Blocker, Alyssa Wong and Rachel Levens.